# Grandfather Counts

by Andrea Cheng
illustrations by Ange Zhang

LEE & LOW BOOKS Inc.  New York

公公 **Gong Gong** (goong-goong): Grandfather

爸爸 **Ba Ba** (ba-ba): Dad

一 **yi** (ee): one

二 **er** (are): two

三 **san** (sun): three

四 **si** (seh): four

五 **wu** (woo): five

六 **liu** (leo): six

七 **qi** (chee): seven

八 **ba** (ba): eight

小孩 **xiao hai** (sheow-hi): children

銀 **Yin** (in): silver

花 **Hua** (hwa): flower

文 **Wen** (when): culture

銳 **Rui** (ray): sharp

很好 **hen hao** (hun-how): very good

Text copyright © 2000 by Andrea Cheng
Illustrations copyright © 2000 by Ange Zhang

LEE & LOW BOOKS Inc., 95 Madison Avenue, New York, NY 10016
www.leeandlow.com

Printed in the United States of America

Book design by Janet Pedersen
Book production by The Kids at Our House

The text is set in Goudy
The illustrations are rendered in acrylic

10 9 8 7 6 5 4 3 2 1
First Edition

Library of Congress Cataloging-in-Publication Data
Cheng, Andrea.
Grandfather counts / by Andrea Cheng ; illustrations by Ange Zhang.— 1st ed.
p. cm.
Summary: When her maternal grandfather comes from China, Helen, who is biracial,
develops a special bond with him despite their age and language differences.
ISBN 1-58430-010-8 (hardcover)
[1. Grandfathers—Fiction. 2. Racially mixed people—Fiction. 3. Language and languages—Fiction.
4. Communication—Fiction. 5. Chinese-Americans—Fiction.] I. Zhang, Ange, ill. II. Title.
PZ7.C41943 Gr 2000
[E]—dc21                                    00-035413

To Grams and Pop
—A.C.

To Neil and Jane, with love
—A.Z.

Gong Gong, Grandfather, was one of the last people off the plane.
He walked slowly toward the crowd waiting at the terminal.

"Ba Ba, Ba Ba," Mom shouted. His eyes lit up as he looked in our
direction. Mom ran over and hugged him. Dad, Henry, Cece, and
I stood back, waiting.

Finally I went closer. Gong Gong patted my head and smiled. Then he said something to me. I looked to Mom for help.

"Gong Gong says you look very nice," Mom explained.

"Thank you," I said.

Gong Gong kept talking to me in Chinese. When he realized I didn't understand, he turned to Mom, a look of surprise on his face. I wanted to explain that Mom had tried to teach us Chinese. She had gotten us Chinese flash cards with words and pictures. Once she sent us to Chinese Sunday school, but we didn't want to go back. The kids there already spoke Chinese. They were learning to write characters, and we couldn't understand anything they said.

On the way home everyone was quiet. Gong Gong dozed next to me. I watched him and wondered what he was dreaming. Did he dream in Chinese?

When we got home, Mom took Gong Gong to his room and shut the door.

"He's tired," she said. "Let him rest."

   It had been my room, a small back room, just big enough for a
bed and small desk. From the window I could see the railroad tracks
that ran along the back of the house to places I could only imagine.
   To get ready for Gong Gong's arrival we had moved my bed into
Cece's room. Her room faced the street. No tracks, no train cars to
count as they sped by.

We put up wallpaper in my room, green with small dots. Mom said it would hide the cracks caused by the rumbling of the trains going by. I missed those cracks, all connected and spreading out from the middle like the branches of a tree in winter.

Mom got upset when the last sheet of wallpaper wrinkled near the ceiling. Dad tried to smooth it with his fingers, but it just creased more.

"It looks okay," I said. "No one will see it way up there."

Mom wasn't sure. "When you do a job, always do it right," she said. "Gong Gong told me that when I was four and he was teaching me to write my name. He said my name was my family. I shouldn't scribble it any old way. But I was little and it was hard to make the strokes of the Chinese characters right."

I got this picture in my head of Mom as a four year old trying to write with a paintbrush full of lumpy wallpaper paste instead of an ink brush. I started to laugh, but I could see Mom didn't think there was anything funny going on.

"Helen," Mom said, annoyed. "Go find something else to do."

Suddenly I felt a lump in my throat. Why was Mom in such a bad mood? All because of Gong Gong?

"Why does he have to come anyway," I cried, "and take my room!"

Mom looked at me, surprised. Then she said quietly, "He's my father. It's my duty to take care of him."

I didn't want to listen. I ran down the stairs, out the door, and down the path toward the railroad tracks.

After Gong Gong first tried to speak to us at the airport, he didn't say much to anyone. Cece drew him a picture of flowers and butterflies. He smiled at her and handed the picture back.

"It's for you," Cece said, but Gong Gong didn't understand. So I taped the picture to the door. Then he understood. He nodded and smiled at Cece again.

"See, he does like it," I told her.

One by one Gong Gong read through the Chinese newspapers he had brought with him. Mom tried to get him to go out, but most of the time he just shook his head and went back to his reading.

"What will Gong Gong do when he finishes all his newspapers?" I asked Mom.

"Give him time," said Mom. "He has so many new things to get used to."

Since I couldn't see the train from Cece's room, I waited for it out back on the concrete wall. Sometimes I saw Gong Gong looking down at me from my old room. Soon I realized he wasn't looking at me at all. He was waiting for the train. When the engineer waved to me, Gong Gong reached out and waved back, too.

Early one evening, I was sitting on the concrete wall waiting for the train when I saw Gong Gong coming down the path. He sat down next to me, his legs hanging over the wall, just like mine.

We could feel the train coming before we heard the low rumble. Then there it was.

"Yi, er, san, si, wu, liu, qi, ba," said Gong Gong, holding up a finger for each car that went by. I liked the way his voice went up and down softly with each word. The engineer waved from the last car and then the train was out of sight.

Gong Gong said the first word again and looked at me, waiting.
I repeated the word, holding up one finger to match his.

"Yi," I said. "One." I got it!

Slowly Gong Gong said all the numbers up to eight and I
repeated them. We started over and practiced until I could say
them all by heart. Gong Gong clapped for me.

Then I held up one finger and said, "One."

"One," Gong Gong repeated after me. Before long he could
count to eight in English.

"You did it!" I said. Gong Gong took my hands in his and gave
them a quick squeeze.

I found a small piece of broken concrete and used it to write HELEN on the wall.

"Helen," I said, pointing to what I had written.

"Helen," Gong Gong repeated, tracing the letters with his finger. Then he picked up a piece of concrete and wrote two Chinese characters on the wall.

"Gong Gong," he said, pointing to the characters. He took my hand and helped me copy his name.

Just then I saw Henry and Cece coming down the path.

"I've called you a million times," said Henry. "Come on. It's time for dinner."

"Sorry," I said. "We didn't hear you. Gong Gong and I were busy."

We walked up the path together. "Yi, er, san," I said, counting my steps.

"Four, five, six," Gong Gong said, continuing where I left off.

At dinner, Dad told us about a new computer program for learning languages. A friend at work had given him a copy of the Chinese version. Dad said it was really great.

"It starts out real simple," Dad explained. "The voice says 'xiao hai' and then you click on the picture of the children."

"Xiao hai," Gong Gong repeated. He smiled and gave Dad a thumbs up. Then Gong Gong looked at me.

"*Three* xiao hai," he said. It was my turn to give him a thumbs up.

"Hey, Mom, what's my Chinese name again?" I asked.

"Yin Hua," Mom replied. "Gong Gong gave you your name when you were born."

"Gong Gong," I said. Pointing to myself I repeated, "Yin Hua."

Gong Gong nodded. Then he pointed to Cece and Henry. "Yin Wen. Yin Rui."

"Hey, we're all Yin something," said Cece.

"Yes, because you're all in the same family," said Mom, "and you're all the same generation."

"Cool," said Henry.

After my bath that night I walked by my old room. There was Gong Gong sitting at the desk. I looked over his shoulder. He was printing HELEN over and over.

"Gong Gong, you're writing my name!" I said.

Gong Gong smiled and motioned for me to sit next to him. Then he wrote some Chinese characters and said, "Yin Hua."

Gong Gong handed me the pen and I tried to copy the characters as best I could. I didn't do a very good job, but then he showed me how to make the strokes in the right order. I wrote my name again and did much better.

"Hen hao," Gong Gong said, squeezing my shoulder.

That meant "very good." Mom always said "hen hao" when I brought home my best work from school.

Gong Gong stood up and went over to Cece's picture on the door. He pointed to a flower and said, "Hua." I understood. *Hua* means "flower." I was Gong Gong's flower!

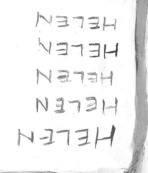

Suddenly I heard the familiar low rumble.

"Gong Gong," I said. We looked at each other quickly and then went over to the open window.

"Yi, er, san, si, wu, liu," I counted.

"Six," said Gong Gong.

"Six cars," I said.

"Six cars," Gong Gong repeated slowly.

The engineer blew the train whistle as Gong Gong
and I waved good night to him together.